Christmas Re-Imagined

Deborah Aloba

First published by Shakspeare Editorial, December 2021

ISBNs   pbk 978-1-9993295-2-5
         ebk 978-1-9993295-3-2

Illustrations © Christine Wong

Design and typesetting www.ShakspeareEditorial.org

Those stories that refer to Jesus Christ and Lucifer being brothers are based on revelations taught by the Church of Jesus Christ of the Latter Day Saints and are based information in: the Bible (Isaiah 14:12; Colossians 1:15); the Book of Mormon and the Doctrine and Covenants (76:25–27; 93:21).

The Stories

1 ∞ Star's Story

Millions of years ago, when I was no more than mere particles in vast clouds of dust and gas, at the beginning of the creation of the universe, God came to me and whispered that he needed me to work on becoming a supernova star. He said that I would need to shine so brightly that my presence would be remembered for thousands of years, even though I would have to die. He told me that he had looked into the heart of two of his children and what he had seen had worried him, and that he might need me to be a special messenger.

I thought about this for a long time. I didn't want to die, but I did want to be a messenger for my God. So could I say no? I thought about what God had asked of me for a long time. During that long period my nebulae remained cold and monotonous. Then I came to life and realised that I did want to be one of God's messengers. I began to rush around excitedly, like a child in park. How could I become a supernova star?

I knew that there were two options: I could streak ahead like a comet or be a shockwave from another distant supernova. I decided to be a comet and began to move with force through the clouds, causing particles to collide, and I began to form clumps. As I continued to move through the universe, my friends nicknamed me Clumpy, because as I got bigger and bigger I created a gravitational pull that attracted even more particle matter from the surrounding clouds.

As more matter fell into my centre, I grew denser and hotter and eventually I formed a small, dense body and became a protostar.

God visited again but said I wasn't big enough yet to be his messenger, but he wanted me to continue working on becoming a supernova star. He mentioned that he was a little concerned that his son Lucifer, who was so named because he was the bringer of light, was becoming rebellious. God had mentioned to him that the inhabitants of one of the worlds he had created, called Earth, were unruly and were not following his teachings. He was concerned that because of their behaviour they would not be able to return to Heaven and live with him at the end of their lives.

Sadly, he explained that he had left his Earth children many messages about what they needed to do to return to him but many had ignored them. The messages were not really very difficult, all they required was that his Earth children be kind towards each other, show empathy and compassion and look after each other. But a lot of them were not doing this, they were cruel and cold towards each other, and some of the things that were done to his smallest and most vulnerable Earth children caused his heart to break.

I asked God why he didn't make them behave properly. He was the creator of the universe and there was nothing that he could not do.

But God explained that his Earth children had to make their own decisions. They had to be given free agency, because if they were forced to do things against their will then they would always resent him, and that resentment would eventually manifest itself in anger and bitterness and Heaven would not be the peaceful place it was at the moment. He said, how could he grant free agency to his children in Heaven and not grant it to his children on Earth? That was why he was worried. When he had expressed his concerns to his son Lucifer, he had replied that God's Earth children would HAVE to obey God. That he would go to Earth and make them behave as God wanted and he would bring them back to God. He had told God that as he was a god in his own right he had the power to do this. He even said that it was his plan to enslave the souls of God's Earth children and make them come back to Heaven.

God told me that he was talking to Lucifer about this. That he was a little concerned because Lucifer had told some of his close friends about his plan and they had agreed with him, but he knew that Lucifer was capable of such goodness, that he was just young and arrogant.

God encouraged me to continue working on becoming a supernova star. So I continued to draw in even more gas and grew even hotter. Eventually I became so hot that my hydrogen atoms began to fuse and to produce helium and I felt an outflow of energy, which was a nuclear fusion. However, the outward push of my fusion energy was still weaker than the inward pull of gravity at this point in my life.

Material continued to flow into me, increasing my mass and making me hotter. Finally, after millions of years, I reached a tipping point and I felt a mass collapse into me, causing two huge gas jets to erupt and to blast the remaining gas and dust clear away from my fiery surface.

It was quite scary, but after a while I stabilised. I felt the outward pressure from my hydrogen fusion now counteract gravity's inward pull and I became a main sequence star. I was growing bigger.

Then God visited me again and said, "I need you to work just a little harder. I am now sure that I'm going to need you. I have looked into Lucifer's heart and I have seen what his intentions are. He now has a small following, but he is intent on gaining more and more followers and eventually is going to try to use them to take away my Earth children's free agency and make them subservient to him.

I have tried and tried to reason with him and I have explained that there are consequences to each action he may take. He pretends to listen and agree with me, but he forgets that I am God and can see into the deepest recesses of his heart and mind.

I could bind him in chains but then I will have taken away his free agency. No Star, my other children and I will continue to try and reason with him and his followers.

You should see his followers, they adore him and he gains strength from that adoration. How can they have forgotten the work we have done together to create realms and worlds?"

I listened, but I did not really understand. I could feel his sorrow. It was so deep and so vast, it made me dim.

Then it was as if he had forgotten my existence. I heard him say, "One of my other children has come to me and told me he is willing to show my Earth children how they can return to me if they want to. I love this child, not more than I love Lucifer, but differently. He is stronger than Lucifer. He thinks of long-term consequences."

God was still as he contemplated the situation. His sorrow was palpable as it flowed from him and washed over me and I grew yet dimmer. Suddenly he came out of his reverie and whispered, "Keep working. I have created you for a purpose. Soon, I think it may be soon."

He left and I felt my strength return. I continued to work, millennia passed and I became as bright as the Sun. During these years I heard rumours about Lucifer becoming more rebellious. Apparently he was a wonderful orator, a charismatic speaker. Although only a few angels had followed him at first, now he had thousands of followers.

Then one day I felt Heaven shake, and I felt the anger and pain of millions of its inhabitants. It was so powerful that it dimmed some of my brilliance. I didn't know what had happened until, a short while later, I heard that Lucifer had gone to God with a plan to bring back the Earth children to Heaven by force. Jesus, his other son, also suggested a plan, that would give the Earth children the choice of returning to heaven or not. God had chosen Jesus's plan over Lucifer's and Lucifer had been furious. Such was his anger at not getting his own way that he had announced he would destroy one of God's most beautiful creations, man, and possibly even Earth itself. So Lucifer had departed Heaven with his followers, a third of the angels.

I didn't believe what I heard at first, but I knew that if it was true, God would come to see me again.

I continued to work and I now shone 20 times brighter than the Sun. I was a Wolf-Rayet star that lit up Heaven. Then one day he was there. I knew because I could feel his pain and had to work very hard to maintain my brightness.

"It is time," he said. "I have lost one son and now I have to send another to Earth. I know Jesus is capable of doing what is right, we have had many discussions, but I don't think he truly understands what I have asked of him. Like all my children, he must be given his free agency, but what if, having experienced Earth, he decides to stay there. It will be a much easier life. He will be revered from the day he is born and with his power he could influence those around him greatly. He could have a wife and children and live a simple life. The price he will have to pay to bring my children who live on Earth back to me will be so great, so painful, that even though he says he is willing, I don't know if I should ask it of him? But then, what will happen to my Earth children? How will they find their way home, if he is not willing to pay the price?"

I stayed silent, but tried to enfold God in the brightness of my rays. After all, he had created me, and I wanted to comfort him.

Suddenly he turned and looked at me. "You have worked so hard and so patiently and I see before me something so beautiful. Now I need you to fulfil the mission I spoke of so many millions of years ago. Are you willing, knowing that you will die much earlier than your allotted time?"

There was no question in my heart, I told him I was willing. So here I am, above a stable where God's beloved son has taken human form as a baby.

I've been here for a while and I've heard the angels sing and I've watched the shepherds come.

I must stay a little longer, until the wise men who are following my path come to greet God's child. Then, as the child grows older and stronger, I will grow smaller and weaker.

Oh! I see them in the distance.

It won't be long now …

2 ∞ God's Story

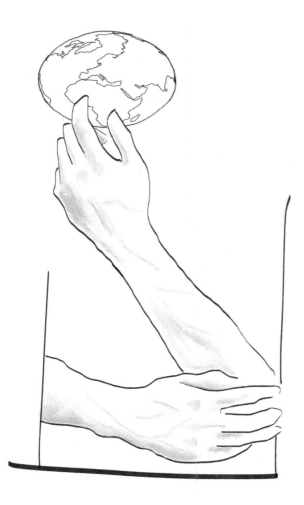

It was with great sorrow that I watched Lucifer, my bright and brilliant son, rebel and finally leave Heaven, angry and bitter, determined to undermine the potential of humans. Determined to bring out the basest aspects of their nature to thwart me. To have a third of my angels leave with him was a blow, especially when I think of them destroying all that they had built up over years and years. But Lucifer was bright and brilliant, a wonderful orator and a persuasive speaker.

How then was I to provide a way for the children I had created on Earth to return to me of their own free will? My children are my blessings. Each one so full of potential. Each one more powerful than they understand or know. Each one individual and beautiful. Each one with their own challenges.

As I pondered the problem Jesus came to me and said that he would be willing to go to Earth and teach my earthly children all they needed to know to choose whether they wished to return to me.

"Jesus, it is not quite as simple as that. Lucifer's actions have changed everything and there are far greater consequences now and the price that has to be paid is much higher."

Jesus sat down next to me, "What is the price?"

I looked at Jesus, so different from Lucifer, with just as much brightness within him but a steadier light. He was much more thoughtful, a child of great compassion and empathy.

I sighed, "The price is beyond what you could imagine." I laid my hand across his shoulder.

Jesus repeated, "What is the price?"

I smiled sadly, "The price is atoning for the sins of each and every person that ever existed on Earth."

Jesus thought for a moment, then said, "I love the Earth children, and I know you love them. I will pay the price."[1]

"Jesus, you have no idea what it will cost you or the level of pain you will have to endure – and I will not be able to help you. I may be able to send my angels to help, but I will not be able to interfere. No, we will find another way."

---

1   Luke 22:43-44

Jesus turned and looked at me and repeated, "I'll pay the price."

"Come with me." I took him to Earth and we walked among my children and I showed him all the cruelty and meaness of humans, but he repeated, "I'll pay the price".

So I took him to the desert and I brought before him 200 men from the outer darkness who had committed the most heinous sins. They had murdered and abused my little ones. They had stolen innocence, destroyed lives and, for a moment, I removed their sins and placed those sins on Jesus. He gasped at the pain, but did not falter. I told him that it was just a small taste of what he would have to endure.

He looked at me steadfastly and said, "I will pay the price."

I brought forth another 300 men who had committed similar sins, which I also placed on Jesus. This time his pain was more evident.

"Jesus, you will need to take on the sins of millions, this is just 500."

He looked at me steadily, unfalteringly, and said, "I'll pay the price."

I removed the sins from him and returned the 500 to outer darkness.

I thought long and hard. Then we walked the Earth again and I showed him babies, then toddlers, children and then teenagers and finally adults.

"This is what you will have to become to fulfil the price." Then I turned him to me and said, "If I agree, it must be on one condition."

He looked at me, "What condition?"

"If you decide to stay with your Earth brothers and sisters, who I know you love, I don't want you feel that you have failed. I want you to know that I love you, no matter what decision you make." I hugged him and whispered, "Remember, you have free will."

So I looked among the inhabitants of the Earth until I found a girl whose lineage was from the House of David. She was pure and honourable. I sent Gabriel to tell her that she had been chosen to be the mother of my son. She agreed, but she was engaged. So I told Gabriel to speak to her fiancé and explain my need for this girl to be the mother of my son.

There was much else to do. The angels needed organising to announce the birth of Jesus to both the humblest and to the most learned of men. Simeon and Anna could be relied upon to confirm not only his birth but also his mission. I had to ensure that Star was ready to shine.

Jesus and I discussed his birth and agreed that he would be born in the humblest of circumstances, so that he would understand what it was to be poor. I remembered that I would need to protect Jesus from Herod. There was so much to do and timing was of the absolute essence.

Now I see him, my son Jesus, God in human form. There he lies, in the most vulnerable and fragile of human forms, a baby. The love I feel for him is magnified. I thought I couldn't feel any more love for him, but I do.

The years ahead are going to be difficult. Unfortunately, he is shortly going to have to escape from his birthplace, with Mary and Joseph, into Egypt. He doesn't realise it yet, but his ministry won't begin for 30 years. And it will end in betrayal and pain, if he has the courage to do what is required to save my children on Earth so that they can return to me. What if he decides the price he has to pay is too high and he changes his mind and decides to live a human life?

I won't think of that now. For now, I will look at my son, held by his mother, protected and loved. His challenges will come, but at this moment he is still and happy and I am so proud of him.

3 ∞ Innkeeper's Story

Well, there's been some odd goings-on lately.
If I told you of some of the things I've seen, you'd
say I'd been drinking my own wine.

A couple of days ago this star appeared in the sky.
It was huge and it lay really low, hanging over the
old stable. Then the girl came with her husband.
She was heavily pregnant. He knocked on my door
asking for a room, saying Miriam had sent him.
What was my sister thinking? A room for goodness
sake! I was full. The census had brought in a
decent bit of trade for once. I told him there was no
room, but he'd pleaded.

There was something about the girl. She reminded
me a bit of my wife when we'd had our first. She
was young, a pretty thing. Something around her
eyes reminded me of Bekah. When I first met
Bekah her eyes were the first thing I noticed. They
were beautiful. This girl looked as if she was going
to have that baby any minute. I could see her biting
her lip to stop herself from crying. Bekah does that.

As for him, I was sure he was a Nazarene. I have family that way.

What could I do? I had to offer them something, even if it was only the old barn. The look on his face was total relief. Anyway, they made their way over. I told Bekah about the girl. Well, you know what women are like. Apart from nagging me that I could have offered them a room. What room, I asked? Was I supposed to magic a room out of thin air? Well, of course she had to go over and check on the girl. I told her it wasn't our business, but she just gave me that look. You know the one? It says, "You're an idiot." No words, but I know what that look means.

She'd only been gone a few moments when she hurried back saying that the girl was going into labour. She rushed past me and grabbed some cloths and told me to look out the swaddling she'd put by for our last child. She'd lost that baby. She hid it well, but she hadn't got over that loss.

I told her I couldn't be looking for swaddling clothes, there was too much to do. She made it very clear what would happen if I didn't help as she slammed the door behind her.

I kept an eye on the barn and eventually I saw the man, I think his name was Joseph, come out of the barn for a minute. The light from that star was really bright and lit up his face. He looked worried.

Then I heard a baby cry, the man went very still. For a moment I thought he might turn away but then I saw him step back into the barn and about half an hour later Bekah came out. She looked thoughtful as she walked back over.

"She alright?" I asked.

Bekah turned to me, "I've never seen a child like it. He's a boy. He's beautiful, with dark hair. And it's like he's filled with light. The man was anxious, wasn't sure about holding him, but she's a natural."

I handed her the swaddling clothes I'd found. She looked at them for a minute and then said, "I'm going to need your help. I want you to move the old manger, there's no crib for the baby."

"Can't he do that?" I asked. "She isn't going to want me around."

Bekah considered that for a minute and then nodded in agreement, "You're right. I'll ask him." Then she was gone.

Well, a couple of days passed and one night I
think I hear singing. I couldn't work out where
it was coming from. It sounded like Heaven. I'd
had a drink, but only the one, and that old star
seemed brighter than ever. Then a whole group of
shepherds turned up and went into the barn. They
were there for quite a while and I could still hear
that singing. Anyway, when they hadn't come out for
a while I thought I'd pop my head round the corner.
All the shepherds were kneeling before the child,
who was just looking at them. He had big eyes.
He was a serious little soul. They were saying that
they'd been told to come and honour him because
he was the child of God, the Messiah.

I thought they were mad. How could a Son of God,
the Messiah, be born in my old stable? I mean to
say, it says in the scriptures:

"Therefore the Lord himself shall give you a sign;
Behold, a virgin shall conceive, and bear a son, and
shall call his name Immanuel. Butter and honey
shall he eat, that he may know to refuse the evil,
and choose the good."[2]

But it doesn't say anything about him being born in
a stable – and especially not MY stable.

---

2   Isaiah 7:14–16

Then the child looked at me, there was something about him that made me feel all calm inside.

The shepherds took their leave a couple of days later and things calmed down a bit. Bekah was over with Mary (that was the young girl's name) a lot, when I really needed her help in the inn. Then Joseph came over, he needed details of our Rabbi, the child needed to be circumcised. I gave him Rabbi Levi's details. He's a bit of a misery, but when he left the child I could see he was a changed person. That child seemed to have a really strong effect on everyone he met.

They asked if they could stay a couple of weeks to let Mary recover a bit. They weren't doing any harm and Bekah was happy, so I agreed. They were still there four weeks later and then the most unusual thing of all happened. Three men arrived with their entourage of bodyguards, servants, camels and horses. It was clear that they were men of importance.

Well, you can imagine what the neighbours said can't you? They wanted to know what was happening, and when they saw that they looked like they had a bit of money they wanted to see if they could sell them bits and pieces. I told them no, they weren't allowed on my property. Simeon Avraham had a right go at me, but it is my property and if I don't want them on it that's my business.

There was no doubt the child was special, and of course there were loads of rumours. Bekah told me the men had kneeled before him and, like the shepherds, acknowledged him as the Messiah. They brought him gifts of gold, frankincense and myrrh. Mary hadn't said much to her, but Bekah said you could see she was a bit overwhelmed but the baby seemed to be taking it in his stride.

Now the little family have gone. Mary knocked on the door in the early hours. She whispered to Bekah that they had to go. They'd received some sort of warning that their child was in danger. I don't know who warned them. I didn't see anyone visit them – and I was up to past midnight.

So, do you believe me? Do you believe that the Son of God, the Messiah of all the Earth, was born in *my* stable? And if you do, why do you believe that he would do that? What's his purpose on this Earth? I'd really like to know.

Whatever it is, that child will heal people's hearts. He healed Bekah's and mine …

4 ∞ Angel's Story

Why wouldn't they let me join the chorus?

Gabriel, he's the head angel you know, sat on the choir panel and every time I auditioned he put his head in his hands and shook it, moaning, "Why do you always sing too loud?"

But I didn't sing too loudly, I just sang joyfully – and I sang in tune. I liked singing God's praises. Gabriel wanted all the angels to sound the same? So boring.

"NO, NO, NO, NO. You cannot join the chorus."

Do you know, I'd had similar comments when I was a human. In fact, I was singing to myself and didn't even see the cart when it hit me. I hadn't realised I was dead. I mean, as far as I was concerned I'd got up and carried on walking, until I realised that I felt a bit lighter than normal. When I looked around I was lying there, with a crowd of people around me.

I stood there watching everyone when suddenly this person was standing next to me. Well, he looked like a person apart from the fact that he had four wings. I thought he was rather handsome.

He told me his name was Michael and he led me into a room where several people were sitting behind a table. They explained that I had died and, having considered my actions on Earth, they had decided that I would be an angel, up until the resurrection.

I asked them when that would be, but no one seemed to know.

That was ages ago and since then I've been given a few jobs to do, you know, passing on messages to people on Earth, protecting people, helping people come to Heaven. But all I really want is to join the choir.

I made some great friends. I've been a bit worried about my friend Rachel. She'd been telling me all this mad stuff that Lucifer had been saying.

When Rachel and I first met she kept asking me what it was like to have a body. She had always been an angel and she really, really wanted a body. She was on the list to go to Earth, but that wasn't for another 300 years and she wanted a body now. Apparently, Lucifer was telling people that if they went with him to Earth they wouldn't have to wait because he would help them find a body and they would be able to feel and touch and experience great pleasure.

Rachel and I had loads of discussions about what Lucifer had said and I tried to explain what it felt like to have a body. I told her that they were more fragile than people thought and that if they were not treated carefully they could be really hurt – and the pain could be unbearable. It was better being an angel, because you didn't feel physical pain, although you still got hurt emotionally. I mean, every time Gabriel said, "NO, no, no, you can't join the choir" it hurt. But I've been here quite a while now and I've never experienced any physical pain.

Lucifer told Rachel that they'd go to Earth to control the inhabitants and make them come back to Heaven. Rachel and I had a long chat about that and how important it was to have free agency.[3] That was one of the best things about Heaven, although I'd died and lived here now, I was still me. I'd always been a bit rebellious and asked a lot of questions; I still didn't like being told what to do. Some of the older angels would get cross with all my questions, but God had told them off and said it

---

3 See Isaiah 14:12–15, Revelation 12:1–17 and Doctrine and Covenants 29:36–37, Moses 4:1–4 Abraham 3:27–28

was important for us to ask questions and not just to accept what other angels said.

Then I heard that there'd been a war in Heaven. I'd been away at the time, trying to help someone on Earth who'd been told they had cancer. I went to find Rachel to ask her what had been happening. But I was told that she'd left Heaven and gone with Lucifer. I couldn't believe it. She wasn't the only one. Loads of angels had gone with him, everyone was upset. God was really sad.

Now I've just heard that Jesus, God's son, has volunteered to go to Earth to try and combat what Lucifer is doing. Apparently, Lucifer wants to destroy God's Earth children out of spite so Jesus is going to Earth in human form to show the inhabitants how they can return to Heaven –and they need a choir of angels to proclaim his birth.

I have to admit that I thought Jesus was a bit mad. I mean, he was a god in his own right, and he was already quite old, but to take human form he was going to have to be a baby! I tried to tell him that he wouldn't have much power as a baby and that he could get hurt. I mean really hurt. I explained that when I was small other children had been mean to me. They had punched and kicked me and my body had really hurt. I also told him about the time I'd fallen over and broken my arm. And about when I got chicken pox and really wanted to scratch. I even explained that it didn't make any difference when you grew up. I'd had a boyfriend who had punched and kicked me, and my mouth had split open, and it had been really painful. Bodies were frail. Jesus had listened patiently be told me he was going anyway. But apparently God had to sort out a few things first, and that would take a bit of time.

I missed Rachel and wondered about her often. Occasionally I saw Jesus and would wave to him. He always waved back, or popped over for a quick chat.

A month before Jesus decided to go to Earth, Gabriel held another audition for a choir of angels who would proclaim his birth.

Of course I went and auditioned and, guess what, Gabriel said yes. Apparently he needed the proclamation to be loud and joyful – and he knew I could do loud and joyful.

So here I am with a host of angels and down below is a group of shepherds. Any minute now we're going to sing our hearts out as we proclaim the birth of Jesus, the Son of God.

5 ∞ Ox's Story

Were *you* there that night?

Right back in the eighth century it was foreseen that I would be present at the birth of Christ. Isaiah mentioned me you know. Just a very small mention, but it was a mention. In Isaiah's first chapter, in verse three, he said that even though men wouldn't recognise Christ, I would. And I did.

For generations, my family had told me that someday something special would happen. None of us really knew what and, you know, I have to admit I'd almost forgotten about it. But, as an ox, not only do I represent the nation of Israel (I bet you didn't know that, did you?), but I also represent patience. And my patience, the patience of all generations of oxen, was rewarded that night.

It had been a really long day. First, I'd been ploughing, then I'd been trampling grain to thresh it. So I was very glad when I was placed in the stable to rest. I was exhausted but I couldn't get much rest because of this huge star that was shining over the stable. It was so bright I could see it even when I closed my eyes.

A bit later, a young girl came into the stable with her husband and a donkey. Donkey settled himself in quickly. He immediately went over to where my straw was and helped himself. That was when I noticed that the girl was heavily pregnant. Well, within the hour she went into labour and we all went very still. When the child was born, I immediately recognised him as God. It was the light you see, he shone even brighter than the stars. But it was also the feeling that entered into me. I didn't feel tired anymore, I felt as energised as when I was a young one. I wanted to kick up and frolic with happiness.

We saw so many things over the next few days. Angels, shepherds and kings. Donkey and I watched over the child. His mother converted the manger that I normally fed from into a crib. Do you know, he hardly cried once? Such a peaceful child. I was sorry when they went.

Were you there that night?

Did you see him?

6 ∞ Donkey's Story

At the time I was born there was a great furore because the Romans had deposed their puppet king Herod Archelaus, and converted his territory into the Roman province of Judea. A few years later (I would have been about three years old), Publius Sulpicius Quirinius (what a mouthful of a name), the newly-appointed governor, was assigned to carry out a census of his new province.

I lived with a man called Joseph and I heard him complaining to his wife Mary about having to register at the census, especially as they were about to have a baby. He wasn't the only one who complained, a lot of his friends were also angry. It wasn't as if they could refuse to go as the censor's power was absolute. Our local rabbi informed everyone that they should go and warned them to not defy the Romans.

I heard Joseph tell Mary that as they belonged to the house and line of David they would have to leave Nazareth and travel to Bethlehem, as that was the province he needed to be registered in. He also told Mary he'd heard that after people registered for the census they were being taxed, and he was worried because money was bit tight!

Mary didn't really want to go. The baby was due shortly and she couldn't face the 65-mile journey in her condition. I could see that Joseph was worried, not only about Mary having to travel, but also because of the rumours about Judas of Gamala. Judas was leading a resistance movement and he was encouraging Jews not to register. If they did register, he ordered his followers to burn down their homes. I know that Joseph felt he was stuck between a rock and a hard place because he'd come and tell me what he was thinking when he was cleaning my stall. But, in the end, he decided to go. That's the thing with humans, they confide in us about so many things. It's a good thing that we don't talk the way humans do, we could cause a lot of trouble if we did.

I remember the day he came into my stable, brushed me down, scratched my ears and told me that I was going to have to help him, because he needed me to carry Mary to Bethlehem. It was a long journey that would take four or five days, but he knew he could rely on me. He put a pannier on me and lifted Mary onto my back. You really wouldn't have known she was there, she was only a little thing. I thought she was quite pretty, and she had always been kind to me.

We set off. There were quite a few of us. I think the idea was that it would be safer to travel in numbers, especially with Judas and his followers on the rampage.

Mary was really sweet and she'd get off my back every so often and try to walk a bit. She'd whisper in my ear, "Donkey, you need a rest too."

Lovely girl.

Every night we'd have to find an inn to sleep in. Some were really a bit rough, but Joseph always made sure I was bedded down correctly and had plenty of hay.

On the fifth day we arrived in Bethlehem. I'd had to carry Mary all day and my back was hurting a bit, but I could sense she was in a bit of pain, so I didn't really mind. We got to Bethlehem at around 2pm, but could we find an inn to stay in? Joseph must have approached 20 innkeepers, but the place was heaving and the prices for the rooms had gone through the roof. Every so often I would hear Mary give a little whimper as if she was in pain. I could see that Joseph was really trying not to panic. He held her hand and told her not to worry, it would be okay. But even I could see that it wasn't going to be okay.

Joseph knocked on the door of yet another inn. When the innkeeper came, he immediately said, "No room, mate." He was a surly old fart.

Joseph mentioned the name of a woman we had met earlier and pleaded with him, "You have to have something. You can see that my wife is exhausted, and she is with child."

The innkeeper sort of grunted and then really looked at Mary. I saw is face soften just a bit. He thought for a minute. "I suppose you could use the old stable. I'll charge you half what I would have for a room."

Joseph said, "We'll take it."

He led me into the stable. A couple of oxen were in there, but it was okay. Nice and clean.

By now it was night, but it looked as bright as day because of this huge star that seemed to have settled over the stable.

Poor Mary was in a bit of a state, I can tell you. Joseph had to lift her off my back. He got her to sit on a bale of hay, but she was moaning. I could see he was panicking as he began putting straw down. Anyway, long story short, the innkeeper's wife popped her head round the door and took over. She helped Mary to have her baby. I'd never seen a child like it. He seemed to exude light from his whole body. Oh, I forgot to say, Mary had a boy and she named him Jesus.

Then a whole load of really weird things happened. I heard these voices singing. They seemed to come from Heaven. And then all these shepherds turned up. And finally these three men, who were dressed really resplendently. They could have been Magi, or even kings. Not that I've ever seen any Magi or kings, but you hear about things don't you?

Anyway, they knelt by Jesus, who was lying in the old manger, which Joseph had turned into a crib. And they left some presents. I know one of them was gold.

All the time that old star just kept on shining.

I was a bit worried about Joseph, there were times he seemed a bit withdrawn, but he was a loving father.

Anyway, we had to stay for about five weeks in all. Then, shortly after the kings came and went, I could feel a sort of presence in the room. I noticed Joseph wake up and he seemed to be listening to someone. He got up really early that morning and told Mary we had to leave. She bundled up everything really quickly. Then Joseph came over to me and scratched my ears and said, "Donkey, I need you to carry Mary and the baby for me again, but this time it's going to be a much longer journey and we are going to have to move fast. We're going to Egypt."

I gave a little whinny, that was miles away. Turned out it was 429.14 miles away!

So, at the moment we're in Egypt. Jesus is a lovely child; we're great friends. He's just beginning to walk properly; I always give a whinny of laughter when he begins toddling towards me and then falls on his bottom. He never cries though, just looks at me and holds out his arms.

Joseph is making a good living as a carpenter and Mary is pregnant again. I'm not sure when we're going back to Nazareth. But I do know that I need to stay near to Jesus. I think he may need me again someday.

7 ∞ Jacob's Story

Jacob stood at the window, watching his uncle's stable at the top of the hill. It had always looked a bit shabby but today it seem to glow. He couldn't explain it. He wanted to go out, but his mother didn't like him leaving the house and the few times he had gone out with her it had been a bit scary because people stared and pointed at him.

Four weeks ago he had gone out on his own without telling his mother, and a group of children had surrounded him and shouted names at him. It had scared him. He hadn't understood why they were so angry, all he wanted to do was play. They'd pushed him from one child to the other, hitting him, and everything had begun to go dizzy. He'd tried to tell them that they were hurting him, but he couldn't get the words out. He just made sounds, sounds no one seemed to understand. He'd fallen down and the stones in the dirt had cut into him, and the dust had gone into his eyes. He hadn't been able to see very clearly, but he had been aware that one of the children was standing over him and was about to raise his foot as if to kick him, and then the boy seemed to fly backwards, away from him. That was when he'd seen the man, who'd looked a little like his dad, kneel down and pick him up. The man's hands had felt just like his dad's and he'd known he was a carpenter.

"Are you okay?" the man asked.

Jacob looked at him but hadn't said anything. The man had taken his hand and led him over to where a donkey stood with a very pretty girl by its side. She looked just like his mother had looked before his baby brother was born.

She held out her hand, "Are you okay? What's your name?"

He wasn't okay, but he couldn't tell her that. The words were in his head but when he tried to say them they came out in a muddle. So he tried not to say anything and the words stayed locked inside him.

She looked at him gently, "You're not okay are you?" She turned to the man, "Joseph, can you get me some water?"

The man fetched the water and handed it to her. The girl pulled out a piece of cloth, dipped it in the water and then she took his hand and gently washed his face. It felt cool. She washed the dirt and dust away from his face and then washed his hands.

"Better?"

He nodded.

She looked at him and said, "Now what are we going to do with you? I'm sure your mother is worried. Where do you live?"

He pointed in the direction of his house.

She turned to man. "Joseph, let's take him back to his home. I'm sure it's not far and I can walk a little way. Put him on donkey."

The man bent down and lifted him as if he was a feather onto the back of the donkey. As they walked towards his house he could see people standing in their doorways, watching them. Their faces were hard, their arms were crossed, and some turned away as they passed. He didn't understand why they did that.

Joseph and the girl walked with him while he pointed to where his house was. He slipped off the donkey and opened the door. His mother ran towards him looking anxious and worried.

"Jacob, I told you not to leave the house."

He pulled her to the door, "Uugh, uugh."

"What is it Jacob?" his mother opened the door and was a little startled to see the man and a girl standing before her.

"Hello, I'm Mary. Jacob was having a little trouble, so we thought we'd bring him home to make sure he was safe."

His mother began to cry. He hated it when she cried. She never cried loudly, just silently as tears fell down her face. He saw his mother look at Mary's tummy, "Please, come in."

Mary glanced at Joseph, "We really shouldn't. We must find somewhere to rest tonight."

Joseph looked at Mary, "You're tired. We can stop for a little while."

Jacob liked Joseph's voice, it was rich and full of patience and kindness. He walked towards him and held out his hand, tugging him into the house.

Joseph smiled. "I have to go and look after donkey."

Jacob gave a little grunt and tugged Jacob harder into the house, indicating that he would get water for donkey.

Mary sat down and his mother brought a jug of water and some Lekach cake. He loved his mother's Lekach cake, she made it specially for him.

"I've told him he mustn't go out, but he gets so lonely. The children have been told he's possessed of a demon, but no child who is so loving could be possessed by anything bad."

Mary nodded, "It's obvious he is a beautiful boy."

"My husband says we may have to send him away, but I can't bear the thought of that." She looked at Mary's tummy again and said, "You're due any day aren't you?"

Mary laid her hand across her tummy, "Yes, any day now. I can feel him kicking. I think he is anxious to come into the world."

Jacob sat next to Joseph listening to the adults talk. After a while Joseph said, "Mary, we have to go. We need to find somewhere to stay."

Jacob heard his mother say, "Go to the inn at the top of the hill. My brother owns it. Tell him Miriam sent you."

Jacob had been sad to see them go, but he'd looked out for them every day. The big star hanging over the stable near Uncle Reuben's inn made it look like it was covered in silver. On the night they'd left he'd heard lots of people singing too. And it had sounded even better than when his Mum sang to him. He really wanted to go and see what was happening at Uncle Reuben's, but his mother had really scolded him the last time he'd left the house without telling her.

He turned to go to bed, but then he heard a jingling outside his house. He went back to the window and saw men on camels, they were wearing very fine clothes and one of them was really dark. He'd never seen anyone that dark. Other men were walking by their side and he could see the glint of their daggers in the moonlight. One of the camels snorted and spat at his window, another made a roaring sound. They were so close he could see their yellow, stumpy teeth.

He watched them go up the hill towards his Uncle's inn until they were almost out of sight. He stood and listened. He could hear his father gently snoring and he was sure his mother was asleep. He wasn't really disobeying. He'd been told that he shouldn't go out in the daytime on his own, but no one had mentioned anything about the night time. He put on his coat and walked over to the door, gently opened it and slipped out and ran after the camel train. No one would notice him among all these people. He just had to be a bit careful because Uncle Reuben might see him, then he'd get scolded again.

He ran behind the stable and slipped in the back way, almost falling over donkey. Then he saw Mary sitting on a bale of hay with a baby in her arms. She was looking at her baby the way his mother looked at him sometimes. Those times when he knew he was loved, even though she scolded him, those times when he felt safe.

Joseph was filling a manger with clean hay. He looked up and saw Jacob. He smiled gently and said, "Hello Jacob. Does your mother know you're here?"

Jacob nodded his head.

"Mmm, well. Maybe you should go back home before she begins to worry?"

Jacob glanced towards Mary. Joseph took his hand gently and pushed him towards her. She smiled and said, "Hello Jacob, would you like to meet my son? His name is Jesus."

The child turned his head to look at Jacob and held out a pudgy hand. Without thinking, Jacob took the child's hand and said to Mary, "He looks like my brother."

Mary looked at him in wonder, "What did you say?"

He repeated the words and then suddenly realised he was actually saying the words. In wonder, he repeated, "He looks like my brother."

Mary stared at him and he thought she looked a little scared. But then he thought he must have imagined it because she smiled at him and said, "I think you should go home to your mother."

He bent down and hugged the child and then ran home shouting words as he ran, to make sure they really were there. He burst into his parent's bedroom and pronounced, "Mary's had a baby and he looks like Simeon."

His parents, startled into wakefulness, thought they were dreaming for a moment. Then Miriam felt Jacob pulling at her, "Come on Mum, you have to come and see Mary. She's had a baby, she called him Jesus and he looks like Simeon."

Miriam fell to her knees and wept.

8 ∞ Shepherd's Story

Reuben and I have been shepherds for so long. I'm almost 60 and it's only now I'm considered to be a good shepherd.

Over the years I've seen many things, but there was a night ten years ago that I still sometimes think could have been a dream. But I know that the things I saw really did happen.

It had been a difficult week. In the mornings, as ever, I led my flock to the pasture, but on two occasions sheep had gone missing. The first was when even the dogs were unable to fight off the wolves who snatched one of my ewes. The other was when two of the sheep prolapsed and I had to try and save them. Of course, I knew there could be a problem. Five of the ewes were in the last month of their pregnancy and that was the time they were most vulnerable to prolapses. I noticed that two had isolated themselves from the flock and had failed to come forward to feed, and they'd seemed in pain. When I checked them, I knew I had to treat them quickly as I could lose both ewes and their lambs. I always carried some sugar with me, and the ewes just needed me to place the sugar on their prolapses to draw the water out of them, causing them to shrink. Once they'd shrunk, I used the flat of my hand to replace them into the correct position.

Luckily, I'd seen Reuben earlier in the day and he'd agreed to look after the rest of my flock while I took care of the ewes. But when I got back, I noticed that another sheep had gone missing. I felt exhausted, and it was late, but I knew I'd have to try to find her. She could easily have fallen into a gully and been unable to pull herself out.

It was an unusually bright night. There was a star I'd never seen before that shone brighter than the moon. The hillside I was searching was lit up as clear as day. I scrambled over the fields, calling to the ewe, and I thought I heard a faint response. I stood still and, yes, like a small breath against my face, I heard her bleating. I walked in her direction, calling and listening, until I could hear her clearly. I could tell from her tone that she was in distress. Eventually I found her. She'd managed to get herself entangled in briars. It took some time to release her and I had to cut off part of her coat, but finally she was free and walked by my side as I returned to the other shepherds.

As I walked over the hill, I saw my friends cowering on the ground. Next to them was a man who was totally illuminated, and tall. Taller than any other man I'd ever seen. He appeared to have wings and there was a bright cloud around him. At first I thought I was dreaming. I was so exhausted, maybe I had fallen asleep. I knew I hadn't been drinking. Sometimes on cold nights I do have a drink, though I'd never let my wife know that. The scene before me reminded me of my old Rabbi standing before the Talmud and reading from the book of Isaiah. What were the words? Oh yes, I remember, "In the year that King Uzziah died, I saw the Lord, high and exalted, seated on a throne; and the train of his robe filled the temple. Above him were seraphim, each with six wings: with two wings they covered their faces, with two they covered their feet, and with two they were flying. And they were calling to one another: 'Holy, holy, holy is the Lord Almighty; the whole Earth is full of his glory'."

I saw Reuben lying on the ground and then I heard the angel speak, "Be not afraid; for behold, I bring you good tidings of great joy, which shall be to all the people: for there is born to you this day in the city of David, a Saviour who is the Christ the Lord. And this is the sign unto you: ye shall find a babe wrapped in swaddling clothes, and lying in a manger."

Then suddenly there were hundreds of angels praising God, and I fell to my knees as I heard them saying, "Glory to God in the highest, and on Earth peace among men, in whom he is well pleased."

The light from those angels was brighter than the most beautiful summer's day and I felt peace fill my heart.

I don't know how long they were there, singing and praising God. I did raise my head to get a better look and there seemed to be hundreds of them. Eventually they left and the sky returned to its black hue and just the light from the star remained. I still wasn't sure that I hadn't been dreaming until I ran towards the other shepherds. It was clear we had heard and seen the same things. We talked about what we were going to do for hours. The angel had told us that a child had been born, but where? The nearest town was Bethlehem, so it seemed logical to start our search there.

Reuben was utterly convinced that this was a special message from God. But Reuben is a more spiritual man than I am and if he hadn't confirmed what I saw I would still have believed I had dreamed the whole thing. We left our sheep, which we'd never done before, ever. But we were all consumed by this need to see if the angel's message was true.

It took us three days, but we eventually found the stable – and there lay the child in a manger. He didn't look like a god, but rather as my own children had looked a few days after their birth. But the light that shone from him and round him, meant there could be no question that a power emitted from this child.

I've never been able to deny what I saw that night. Many who we told about our experience considered us mad and accused us of drinking. But I know I saw angels. And they did proclaim to us the birth of Christ. And I did kneel before him in a stable.

Reuben and I meet up every so often to talk about what we saw. Somehow it changed us. I hadn't realised there had been bitterness in me, an anger, but it dissipated that night.

You know, the funniest thing was, we were gone for a week and when we returned we hadn't lost a single sheep.

9 ∞ Mary's Story

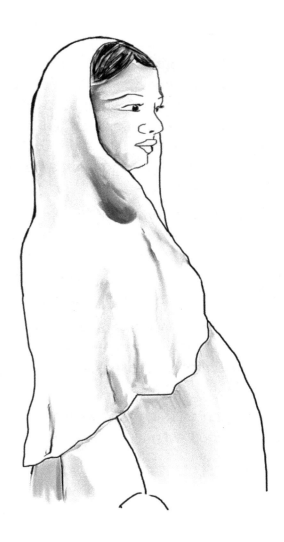

Joseph has been so good, but then I
always knew he was a good man. Coming back
from my visit to Cousin Elizabeth had been hard.
When I'd first seen her I was amazed. She was
well past child-bearing years and yet she'd been
noticeably pregnant.

She explained that an angel had appeared before
her husband, Cousin Zacharia, and had told him
that she would bear a son, who they would name
John. And that he would be a joy and a delight and
that he would be great in the sight of God. Cousin
Zachariah had been unable to speak since he had
seen the angel.

She had been doubtful, but she had become
pregnant, despite her age, and the baby was due in
four months.

It had been such a relief to be able to tell her what
had happened to me, and to be believed. She didn't
question what I said. It had been Mum's idea to
send me to see Cousin Elizabeth. Mum was the
only other person I had told about the visit from the

angel and what he had said. She'd been kneading bread when I told her and I saw her body tense as she realised what I'd said. Then, for a moment, she'd looked at me as if I had gone slightly mad, but she knew I wasn't a liar. She sat down with me and held my hand. We discussed what had happened and what I was going to do.

The biggest worry was Joseph, to whom I was engaged. Of course I was worried about everything else, but it wasn't until I began to discuss the situation with Mum that I realised how much I loved him. Joseph was a few years older than me and loved by my parents. He created the most beautiful work out of wood. Yes, he made shelves and cupboards and all the things that carpenters make, but he took such care of the details that there was beauty within his work. He had shown me some other pieces he had created, one of them was a carving of me. Joseph didn't say much, but he expressed his love for me in a myriad different ways. How could I tell him? How could I watch the look on his face as that love was replaced with shock – and possibly hate? Although he was a kind and tolerant man, I had a funny feeling that his kindness and tolerance would not stretch to believing that I had been visited by an angel who had told me I would become pregnant. Joseph always treated me the greatest respect, but I knew that he desired me. He was going to think I had been intimate with another man.

Mum's idea that I visit Elizabeth had been genius. She'd said it would give me time to absorb all that had happened and work out how to tell Joseph. She'd pointed out that in the end I might have to move in with Elizabeth permanently. If Joseph couldn't accept my explanation then he would have the right to declare me an adulteress, even though we'd not had our wedding ceremony, and that could result in my being stoned to death. I hadn't even considered that. I could almost see the cogs of Mum's brain whirring away as she tried to think of a solution. She promised that, no matter what, she wouldn't let them kill the baby or me, but I might have to leave the family permanently.

Anyway, Mum sent me to Elizabeth, who was amazing. She was so welcoming and we sat for hours, discussing these children God wanted us to give birth to. But it was different for Elizabeth. She was married and Zacharia wasn't going anywhere. He had been the one who'd seen God's angel. I questioned why God hadn't sent an angel to Joseph, that would have solved everything. At three months I began to show. The problem with being small was that if I put on just a couple of pounds it was easily visible. I began to wear looser-fitting dresses. Then a letter came from Mum saying that I needed to return, things had to be sorted out with Joseph. I didn't really want to leave Elizabeth, I'd felt so safe with her. But Mum was right, Joseph needed to know and Mum was building up the courage to tell Dad.

As I travelled back home I began to realise the enormity of the situation. Even though I'd prayed about it a lot I couldn't see how to resolve the matter. Who was going to believe that an angel had visited me and told me I would become pregnant with God's child? If someone had told me such a story I wouldn't have believed them. I'd have thought they were making an excuse to cover up the fact that they'd had sex with someone other than their fiancé.

I wasn't even sure Mum would be able to save me if Joseph decided to inform the Rabbi and the elders that I had been unfaithful. Then there was my family. They would have to live with the shame I had brought upon them forever. It would kill my Dad.

I had hoped to speak to Joseph and try to explain before he noticed. But he came round earlier than I had expected and I hadn't been wearing the loose-fitting dress when he'd arrived. I'll never forget his look of disbelief when he saw me. He didn't shout, or make a huge scene. Maybe it would have been easier if he had. He just looked devastated and his voice was full of such sorrow as he questioned me.

I told him about the angel appearing before me and repeated word for word what he'd said: "Hail, thou art highly favoured, the Lord is with thee; blessed art though among women." Also, that he'd told me I shouldn't be frightened because I had "found favour with God" and that I would "conceive in my womb, and bring forth a son", and that I would have to "name that son Jesus".

I explained to Joseph how the angel had told me that this child would be great, and that he would be called "the Son of the Highest: and would reign over the house of Jacob for ever; and of his kingdom there would be no end".

Joseph had looked at me as if I was mad, and then he'd become angry and told me that he didn't like being lied to. Even when he was angry he didn't shout. I almost wanted him to shout.

I said that I'd explained to the angel that we weren't married yet. But all the angel had said was that the Holy Ghost would come upon me and that this child would be holy and would be called the Son of God. And that it wasn't just me. My cousin Elizabeth, who was in her sixties, was also pregnant. Her husband Zacharias had been told that their child would also be great and I told Joseph their story. I was crying now, but the look on his face told me he didn't believe me. Then he turned away and left. I couldn't blame him.

Mum came over to me after she saw him leave and I just sobbed and sobbed. I didn't know what to do. Neither of us knew whether he would decide to report me to the synagogue leaders. Mum wanted me to leave there and then, but I was exhausted and we decided to wait until early morning.

I began to pack some clothes and my hand went to the carving Joseph had made of me and I started crying again. Mum tried to comfort me, but where was God? How could he give me this responsibility and not provide a way?

There was a knock on the door and Joseph walked in. Mum looked at him, gave a small nod and walked out. I knew she wouldn't go far.

Joseph looked at me and told me that he was going to annul our engagement. He wouldn't tell anyone I was pregnant but he thought it would be a good idea if I went away. And then he left. I collapsed into a chair.

Mum came back in and I told her what he'd said. I saw the relief on her face. She gave me a hug and put me to bed, but I didn't sleep. I prayed all night, but I have to admit I had given up hope.

I was just finishing my packing when Joseph returned the following day and said that he'd also been visited by an angel who had reassured him that everything I had said was true and that he would marry me and grant me his protection from that moment on.

On the day of our marriage I am sure I felt the baby kicking within me, as if he was happy. Mum said that wasn't possible because I was only about 14 weeks along and you couldn't feel babies kicking until they were about 17 weeks along. But I am sure I felt him kicking.

We settled down to married life, but it was a bit odd because we weren't intimate with each other, not in that way, but in so many other ways we became closer and closer.

Joseph was busy with work and I was busy at home. Mum helped me and tried to prepare me as much as she could. I was so glad she was going to be with me when I had the baby. Then a decree went out from Caesar Augustus that there was to be a census about four weeks before the baby was due. Joseph disliked the Roman rule as much as anyone but Rabbi Levi persuaded him to attend the census. Because we were both born under the lineage of David we were going to have to travel to Bethlehem, which would take at least five days. Joseph said that I should stay home, but I knew that would get him into trouble, so I told him I'd be okay. I didn't let on that I was worried by how soon the baby was due.

It was a difficult journey, even riding donkey. When you're heavily pregnant you need to go to the toilet a lot and there weren't that many inns along the way. To be frank, I'd been in pain and was worried about the baby. Joseph was so patient, but I could tell that he was worried too.

By the time we got to Bethlehem, it was heaving with people. Joseph tried so hard to get us a proper room, but every inn he went to was full. It wasn't that we couldn't pay, it was simply that Bethlehem was jam-packed. We were turned away from so many inns that Joseph decided to try to find a room in an area we didn't know very well.

As we turned down an unfamiliar road, we saw a child on the ground surrounded by a group of children chanting "possessed, possessed". One of the group was about to kick the child on the ground and, before I knew it, Joseph had run forward and thrust him away, the other children ran off. Joseph bent down to the boy to make sure he was alright. I always knew Joseph would be a good father but in that moment I realised that he would be a wonderful one.

We made sure the boy was alright and dropped him back to his mother, a kind woman called Miriam. She invited us into her home for refreshments. I was grateful for the chance of a rest, especially as she mentioned that an inn at the top of the hill was owned by her brother, and that if we mentioned her name he might be able to rent us a room.

As donkey carried me up the hill I felt a sharp pain that caused me to gasp and grab Joseph's hand. Eventually the pain subsided.

Joseph knocked on the door of the inn and explained that Miriam had sent us.

The innkeeper scowled and said, "I don't know why she sent you here. I'm full. I haven't got a room."

Joseph pleaded, "Please, you must have something. You can see my wife is heavy with child."

The innkeeper looked at me for a long time and then jerked his head towards a stable and said, "You can go in there."

I felt another stab of pain and gasped. Joseph hadn't argued and just said, "Thank you."

I'd been really worried. Mum had described this pain to me and it looked as if my contractions had started, but they couldn't have because I knew I wasn't due for another three weeks. Also, Mum wasn't with me and in my wildest imaginings I hadn't believed that I would be having my baby in a stable. I'd been convinced that the contractions would stop, but they didn't. I turned to Joseph and said, "I think the baby's coming."

I saw the worry in his face as he lifted me off donkey and onto a bale of hay. He clasped my face in his hands and said, "Don't worry."

He quickly laid down straw and placed a blanket on top. Then I felt my waters break and I grabbed at him and said the baby was coming and that I wanted my Mum. That was when there was a knock and a woman walked in.

I was gasping for breath. She came over and laid her hand against my stomach and then she turned to Joseph and said, "I need to get some cloths. Stay with her." And he did. When she came back she'd pushed him out of the door, and then told me what to do.

I don't know what we would have done without Rebekah. She stayed with me until he was born, this child of mine, and she explained how I should breastfeed. Then she'd called Joseph back in and handed Jesus to him as she helped clean me up. She couldn't know that he was Jesus's stepfather, or that we'd never been intimate, or that I had felt embarrassed as he handed Jesus to me to be fed. Rebekah eventually left and Joseph had stayed by my side.

We had a really long talk about the way forward and how we were going to manage the situation. He was really honest regarding his concerns about what sort of stepfather he might be. I told him that he was a good man and that I knew he'd be a wonderful stepfather. I knew I was lucky to have a man that God put so much faith in. Joseph had been chosen, just as I had been chosen, to be a parent to this child. What greater honour could we have been given?

It took me a while to recover from the birth and Joseph was very protective. I enjoyed just being Jesus's Mum for two whole days before the visitors began to arrive.

In the first week, it was the shepherds. They told us that angels had announced the birth of the Son of God. Apparently, when they'd first seen the angels they'd been really scared, but they'd been directed to come and see my child. As they knelt before him I noticed that Jesus seemed to radiate an energy and light that he directed towards them. A sense of peace seemed to emanate from him and I could feel it transfer to the shepherds. As I watched, I wondered what I would be able to give this child of mine.

Two weeks after the shepherds left, we took Jesus to the temple for the ceremony of redemption. We bought two doves and offered them up as a sacrifice to God. We were preparing to leave when an elderly rabbi approached us and introduced himself as Simeon. Then he did something really unusual. He asked to hold Jesus and he raised him up reverently and said, "Lord, now lettest thy servant depart in peace, according to thy word; for mine eyes have seen thy salvation, which thou has prepared before the face of the people; a light for revelation to the Gentiles and for glory to thy people Israel." And then he told us of the greatness of Jesus's mission. His words worried me a bit.

Jesus was back in my arms and we began to walk out of the Temple when a woman approached and introduced herself as Anna. I later found out she was a prophetess.

She also took Jesus from me and acknowledged him as her redeemer and testified to both of us of his greatnesss. It was all a bit overwhelming.

We returned to the stable and began to prepare to go home. But shortly after we were visited by three men and their entourage. Joseph said they were Magi. I just know that I heard a knock at the stable door and when I opened it I was startled to see a young man in very fine clothing. Behind him I glimpsed three men who looked like kings, not that I had ever seen a king.

They had a large entourage and so many camels and horses. One of the kings, I think his name was

Balthasar, told us that they had followed a star, which had led them to Jesus.

When they saw him they fell to their knees and worshipped him. We hadn't been sure what to do or what to think, especially when they gave us the gifts. Gold, frankincense and myrrh. I didn't understand why they'd given us myrrh – everyone knows it's used at funerals.

It was all too much to take in at the time. I just wanted to sit down and think it all through. So much has happened since Jesus's birth. At less than five weeks old we've seen him acknowledged as the Son of God by shepherds, wise men, rabbis and a prophetess.

Then Joseph told me he'd had a dream and that we had to leave immediately because Jesus was in danger and so we had to escape.

His safety is such a responsibility and I feel overwhelmed, but there is no time. Joseph is our protector. We have to go on another long journey and we have to trust in God that we will arrive safely.

We will be strangers in a strange land, but we have faith that God will protect us.

10 ∞ Joseph's Story

We'd been travelling for hours. Mary was exhausted and I'd knocked on the door of so many inns. All the way on the journey I had run over and over in my mind what had happened over the last few months.

It had been agreed for several years that I would marry Mary. She came from a good family and we were well matched, but that wasn't the reason that I was going to marry her. I loved her. Yes, she was younger than me, but there was a stillness about her. She was beautiful, not just physically, she was kind and thoughtful and very bright – and she had a quite suprising, wicked sense of humour

I was surprised when she'd told me she wanted to go and see her cousin Elizabeth shortly before our marriage, but I wasn't particularly concerned. Although she had seemed a bit on edge.

She'd been gone quite a while, almost four months. I was looking forward to seeing her. I hadn't realised how much a part of my life she'd become.

I decided to surprise her by finishing work early and popping round to see her, but it had been me who'd received the surprise. As I walked in the door I could see she'd put on a bit of weight, but when I looked at her really closely it dawned on me that she was pregnant. At first I thought I was imagining things, I knew there were other men who would have liked to have been her betrothed. When I looked again she was putting on a coat over her dress and then I looked at her face and I could see she was worried.

She asked me to sit down and then told me some ridiculous story about being visited by an angel who had told her that she would become pregnant and would bear the Son of God. I just looked at her. The hardest thing was that she seemed to believe what she was saying. I was too shocked at first to be angry, but then I looked at her and thought she had to have been with another man. She had betrayed me. I was filled with anger. I couldn't stay in that room, knowing that she'd been with someone else. I had to go. And so I went to the forest, where it was cool and I could think. Being among the cedars's spicy scent always made me feel calmer.

I hadn't known what to do. In a flash of anger I considered letting the rabbi and religious leaders know what she had done. I knew they wouldn't argue if she was taken to the square and stoned to death. I knew I wouldn't do that, but it hurt. I'd thought that I had found my soulmate but I couldn't marry her now. I stayed in the forest all day, thinking. When I returned I'd gone to see her. She'd looked ill and it was clear that she'd been crying. I wasn't able to look at her as I told her that I couldn't marry her. She slumped into a chair as I left.

I didn't sleep that night. I tossed and turned. Then just before dawn my room filled with a white light. I turned to see where the light was coming from and found a man standing by my bed. He was full of light and his face shone. At first I thought I was dreaming but then he called me by my name. I put out my hand to touch him and to make sure I was not dreaming and immediately felt totally calm.

Then he said, "Joseph, son of David, do not be afraid to take Mary home as your wife, because what is conceived in her is from the Holy Spirit. She will give birth to a son, and you are to give him the name Jesus, because he will save his people from their sins."

He confirmed what Mary had told me, that indeed she had been chosen to bear the Son of God. He told me that I needed to support her and marry her. There are times in your life when something so startling happens that it changes the course of your life.

I'd decided that I wouldn't marry Mary. It hadn't been a decision I had taken lightly but in that moment everything changed.

I washed and dressed and immediately went to see her. I told her what had happened and we set the date for our wedding, which went ahead shortly afterwards.

She's a good wife, but I thought it was a mistake to bring her with me to the census. I shouldn't have let her persuade me. With Judas of Gamala on the prowl with his thugs the journey hadn't been particularly safe. He calls himself a revolutionist, fighting the Roman oppressors, but he has become an oppressor by burning our homes because we comply with Roman laws. And now I couldn't find anywhere for us to stay and she wasn't saying anything, but I could see she was in pain. I just hoped Miriam's brother had space.

We plodded on up the hill and I could see lights on at the inn. I was thinking, "God, where exactly are you? This is your child and yet you seem to have abandoned us. Surely you know our situation?"

I knocked on the door, and the innkeeper came. Yet again I asked if there was any room at the inn. He said no. It told him that Miriam Levi said that he would have a room.

"Well, I haven't."

I took a breath and said, "Please, my wife is exhausted."

His eyes flicked to Mary and widened as he saw how heavily pregnant she was. His eyes moved to her face and he seemed to soften a little. He didn't say anything and I stayed still. I could see him thinking. Then he tipped his head towards the right and said, "You could go in there."

It was a stable covered in a light that seemed to be coming from a huge star hovering above it.

"Thank you."

Mary whimpered and I led donkey into the stable and lifted her down onto a bale of hay. I was at a bit of a loss but I couldn't let Mary know that so I took her face in my hands, pushed her hair out of her eyes and said, "It's going to be okay."

Then the miracle happened. The door opened and in walked a woman who looked a bit like Mary. She said, "My husband says your wife looks like she is about to give birth. Do you need any help?"

I felt as if all the air had been knocked out of my body – the relief.

Mary moaned and the woman went over to her, "I'm Rebekah." She placed her hand on Mary's stomach and looked at me, "Stay with her. I need to get some things."

She seemed to have been gone for hours but it could only have been minutes. She smiled at me reassuringly and then gave me a little push towards the door. Mary whimpered again and I walked outside where it was as bright as daylight. I could hear singing. People were praising God in the highest, but they sounded as if they were above me.

It had been a while since I'd thought about what the birth of Jesus would mean, but now I felt overwhelmed. How was I going to be a parent to the Son of God? What could I teach him? I had hoped that if I had a son he would become a carpenter like me and my father, but this baby wouldn't be *my* son would he? How could I be expected to bring him up? Thought after thought chased through my head, but nothing really made sense, especially with the singing. I don't know how long I was there before I heard his cry. So, it had begun.

I waited and quite a while later Rebekah opened the door and called me in. I walked over to Mary. The baby was at her breast. When I approached I could have sworn that he stopped feeding and looked at me, but it must have been my imagination. I could see he was strong.

When he finished feeding, Rebekah took him from Mary and placed him in my arms. This time I wasn't imagining that he was looking at me. This child was full of a power I could feel. So again, I questioned what it was I could give him.

Rebekah left us and Mary and I talked about our concerns. She reminded me that in his present state this child, this God, was no more capable of coping without our protection than any other child. Yes, we could feel he was filled with power but at this stage of his life within a frail human body, all that power was limited. Anyway, she told me, she needed me and the more we'd been together the more she had learned to love and respect me. I knew she was telling the truth. I don't think anyone could be in the presence of Jesus and not tell the truth.

Two days passed and we were slowly adjusting to being parents. Jesus was a good baby, but he liked to feed. God or no God he had a good earthly appetite, and, for the most part, a contented disposition.

I was finding it difficult to sleep. The stable wasn't dark at night because of the huge star that hung above it and the constant singing. We were both getting tired.

Around 9pm the day after Jesus's birth, I heard voices outside the stable. At first I thought it was the innkeeper and Rebekah, but the voices all sounded male and they were going to wake up Mary and Jesus. I went to the door to ask whoever it was to be quiet. Before me was a group of shepherds, there must have been 20 of them. I asked if they could be quiet. One of them stepped forward and introduced himself as Reuben. He said an angel had told them to come to see the child.

I asked "What child?"

He replied, "The Messiah. the Saviour of the World."

In other circumstances I would have thought he'd been drinking, but hadn't I seen an angel, and couldn't I hear loud singing that was proclaiming the birth of the Son of God? That was when the enormity of what was before Mary and me truly hit me. I told them to wait and went to Mary, who had woken and was singing a lullaby to Jesus. I told her what the shepherds had said and she looked at me and gave a little nod, and I went and let them in.

The moment they saw him they knelt before him. Small as he was he seemed to understand and his whole being seemed to give off light. It was a bit unnerving if I'm honest. I could see that the power this child emitted would grow and grow and the question that kept going through my head was, "Why would God allow his son to be born in a stable? Why?" I couldn't make sense of it.

The shepherds stayed quite a while and throughout Jesus looked at them with his arms spread towards them. Babies aren't supposed to see when they are born, well not clearly, but it was obvious that Jesus could. As for the shepherds, it was as if they were under a spell. Eventually they did leave, but I knew they would be back – and they were the following day. In the end I could see it was exhausting Mary, so I had to explain that they needed to go back to their families. But they still lingered for a while. Mary didn't say much but I could see that she was thinking, you could always tell because she bit her upper lip.

Shortly after I arranged for the rabbi to come and circumcise Jesus. He didn't like it and I think he found it painful. His face screwed up and he yelled in protest. I could see that there was a bit of a temper in this child.

The next 12 days were peaceful and gave Mary time to recover from the birth. We were getting used to sleeping in the light because that star was still hovering above the stable.

We went into town to give an offering to God and there was an incident with Rabbi Simon, I think that was his name. We'd been walking out of the temple when he approached us and took Jesus out of Mary's arms. He declared that he'd seen the Saviour of the World and could now die in peace. Then a woman, who announced that she was a prophetess, said much the same thing. Mary commented that she hoped that it wasn't going to be like this all of Jesus's life.

We still had to attend upon the Roman authorities and register for the census, so we decided to stay for a couple of weeks so that Mary could fully recover.

It was four weeks later when I heard clanging and snorting outside the stable. There was a knock and when I opened the door there was a young boy in a brightly coloured uniform. Behind him was a large entourage. I could see three elderly men in beautiful clothing being helped off their camels. They seemd to be surrounded by a small army and people from the inn had come outside to see what was going on.

The young boy announced that his master had followed the star for many miles to see the holy child. For a moment I didn't know what to say or do. Then the oldest man came forward and smiled and gently explained that they wished to see the child. He didn't seem to be worried that he was coming to a stable. I explained that I would just have a quick word with Mary. I had to make sure she was prepared for this and eventually I let them in.

They acted in exactly the same way as the shepherd's had. The only difference was that they presented Jesus with gifts of gold, frankincense and myrrh. I noticed that Gaspar was quieter than his two companions and he asked to hold Jesus.

They said they had been dreaming of this moment since they'd been young men. They told us about their journey and their families. They were all astronomers and, in their own countries, were called Magi.

Mary didn't say much, she just listened and occasionally she held my hand. It was quite surreal really. Here we were, a carpenter and his young wife from a small town called Nazareth, sitting in a stable and talking as equals to Magi. Yes a stable, where the Son of God had been born.

Eventually they left, and Mary and I prepared to go home. We were going to stay another couple of days just to try and make sense of everything that had happened. Finally the star had moved and the singing had stopped, although I'd got quite used to it by now. We'd gone to bed and I was in a deep sleep when I was woken up by the same angel who had reassured me about marrying Mary.

He said, "Take the child and his mother and escape to Egypt. Stay there until I tell you to leave, for Herod is going to search for the child to kill him."

I've woken Mary up and we have to go – and go now. She is packing frantically and I can see she is really worried. But Jesus is asleep and totally oblivious. I think my role is to protect Mary and Jesus and I can and will do that.

Mary is asking me about her mother and how we can let our families know what has happened to us. She is saying we don't know anyone in Egypt and she wants to know if it is really necessary for us to go. After all, if we go back to Nazareth Herod won't bother with such a small town. I ask her if she wants to take that risk and she holds Jesus to her protectively and sadly says no.

She points out that we don't have any money. Well, not enough for us to survive on. I point out we have the gold from the kings and that God has prepared the way.

We run out of the stable, looking around to make sure that we are safe. I hold Jesus while she quickly runs to Rebekah to say goodbye.

Then she gets on donkey and takes Jesus back into her arms.

Now, quietly, we begin our journey to Egypt. It may be my imagination but we seem to be following a star, could it be the same one that stood above the stable for so long. We have faith and we will do all we can to protect Jesus, our child, God's child.

11 ∞ Stable's Story

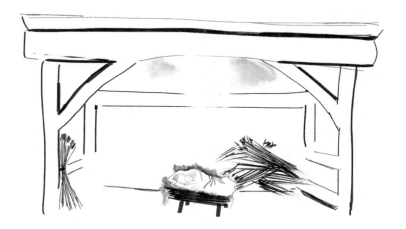

When I first saw them, the innkeeper was really quite cross, he didn't seem to care that the young girl was heavily pregnant, or that her husband looked exhausted. All he was doing was saying, "No, no, no, there's no room here."

The young girl turned to her husband and said, "Joseph, I'm so tired. What are we going to do?."

The man turned to her, smiled gently and said, "Don't worry. It'll be okay."

He turned back to the innkeeper, "Miriam said you would have a room. Have you nothing, something, anything? The smallest room will do. You can see that my wife is due to have a baby. We've been to so many inns and they're all full."

The innkeeper looked at the young woman and his face softened slightly as he said, "Well, I suppose you could stay in the stable."

The young woman groaned. At first, I thought it was because of the thought of her having to spend the night in me, but then I saw the worried look on Joseph's face, "We'll take it."

I watched as Joseph led the young woman towards me, "It will be okay Mary."

She gave another groan and held his hand tightly, "I'm scared Joseph, I think the baby is coming and it isn't due for another two weeks, I thought I'd be at home when the baby came and Mum would be with me."

"Don't worry, I'm with you. Look, someone has left some new hay in here and it's a sturdy little building. I just have to find a way of making sure that you can have some privacy."

The innkeeper's wife put her head round my door, "My husband mentioned that your wife may be going into labour. Do you want some help?"

The relief on Joseph's face was obvious, he said, "We would be grateful. Is there any way we can just cover up the top section of the barn door so that my wife has a little more privacy?"

"Leave it with me." She went over to Mary. "How often is the pain?"

"Every ten minutes."

"I'll be back. I think I have some swaddling from when I had my last child."

Mary went to thank her, but she as she opened her mouth she groaned again.

Joseph took her hand and led her over to a bale of hay in my left-hand corner. "You need to sit down just for a minute while I clean up this old stable."

I have to admit I was a little miffed. I wasn't that dirty. And anyway I was providing him with shelter for the night.

He took an old broom and began sweeping my floor. Obviously donkey and ox had been a bit messy, so I suppose he had a bit of a point. He did a great job mucking me out and then he laid down some of the new straw. Then he went over to the donkey who'd been carrying Mary and took a blanket from one of the panniers and laid it on top of the straw. He then filled up a couple of buckets with water. Mary had been making small whimpering sounds for a while, he went over to her and gently took her face in his hands, "Look at me."

She had huge brown eyes and now she had removed her headdress, I could see she had long brown hair and was young. I had thought she was older. He was at least 30.

"Look at me."

She raised her face.

"It's going to be fine. I need you to get up and come and lie on the blanket."

"I can't Joseph, I'm in too much pain."

So he bent down and picked her up as if she were no more than a feather and carried her over to the blanket.

The door opened and the innkeeper's wife walked back in. It was then I noticed the most enormous star I'd ever seen – and I've been in this same spot for many years and I know about stars. I'd never seen one like this. It seemed to shine right above and through me. It made my old grey-brown timbers glow with a silver light.

"How's she doing? I don't think it will be long. I'll look after her."

Joseph stroked Mary's face, "I'm here if you need me, don't worry."

He turned to the innkeeper's wife, "I'm sorry, you didn't tell me your name."

"Rebekah."

He turned back to Mary, "Rebekah is going to help."

Mary put her hand up to his face, "Thank you for always being there for me."

He smiled and whispered so that only she could hear, "I love you and I'll always be here for you."

She groaned and Rebekah gently pushed him out of the door.

Mary continued to moan with pain and her cries got louder and louder. Suddenly there was a moment of stillness and then we all heard a baby cry.

Rebekah turned to Mary, "It's a son. You have a son." She settled Mary down and then went out and called Joseph, who walked slowly into the stable.

Joseph looked at Mary and the child. He went over and took her hand, "You okay?"

She nodded and then the child looked at him. Yes, I could have sworn he looked directly at him and smiled and stretched out his hand. Just for a moment Joseph held his breath. He seemed to be thinking, and then he smiled and enfolded the child's hand in his own. He looked over at Mary and said, "Your son."

I did wonder about that *your* son, not *our* son.

He went to move his hand and the child grabbed his finger and wouldn't let go. Joseph smiled and said to Mary, "He's strong. Perhaps he'll be a carpenter after all."

I had never seen a child like it. He seemed to radiate with light. He settled quickly against Mary and fell asleep.

Then things got really odd. I could hear singing, really beautiful singing. It went on for hours. It made people come out of their homes and look at the sky in wonder. I can tell you, the Bethlehem choir does not sound like that.

And then all these people kept coming to see the child. In all my years I'd never seen so many different people. Shepherd after shepherd came and knelt before the child, calling him the Saviour. I heard them say that they'd been told to come and see the child by an angel, but I must have misheard that bit. One even left a lamb.

All the while the child radiated this light. Joseph seemed to withdraw a little and Mary seemed a bit overwhelmed. And every night the star stayed right over me. It actually made me look young and beautiful.

Rebekah popped in every day. I know she was a bit shocked about all the happenings, but she loved that child. She said she'd never seen a child like it, so content, so easy. She and Mary talked for hours and she was always showing Mary little tips about looking after the baby.

I got really attached to that family. For a couple of nights it was cold and I tried really hard to stretch my wooden slats so that all my cracks and holes disappeared and I could keep everyone warm. It was a bit of strain but somehow I wanted to protect them. On warmer nights those cracks and holes would let in a soft breeze.

More than once the light from the star stole into the stable and lit up the child's face. He never woke, he was a good sleeper. Mary had good singing voice and would sing lullabies to him.

There was a bit of lull for two, or was it three, weeks and then these three men came with all their camels and horses. There wasn't room in me for all of them. Though, of course, Joseph and the innkeeper made sure they had plenty to drink and they settled down around me without any fuss. I'd never seen anyone as grand as the men. They entered me to see the child and to kneel before him and call him Messiah (I don't know what one of those is).

Well, you should've seen Joseph. I think it unsettled him a bit. Mary seemed quite calm though, well, until they gave the child the presents of gold, frankincense and myrrh. She kept rolling the bottle of myrrh in her hands and then she hid it at the bottom of the pannier. I could see how everything that was happening was really making her think.

It was interesting listening to the men talk about their journey following the star and about their astronomy. Normally, it's just Ox telling me about his day ploughing, or the innkeeper having a moan as he cleans me.

Then men left yesterday and last night Joseph woke Mary up and said that they had to get out immediately. They packed up really fast. Mary knocked on the inn door and hugged Rebekah before climbing onto the donkey's back with the child.

I watched them ride away. I hadn't realised until he was gone how much light the child had brought into me – and not just from that star which, by the way, has now disappeared, but from himself.

I don't know where they are going, but I do know that child has divinity within him.

I wonder if I'll see him again?

12 ∞ Gaspar's Story

Melchior, Balthasar and I studied the

stars for years. Even as young boys we'd been fascinated by the stars and the messages and stories within them.

Melchior, my cousin, was best at interpreting them. His father, like mine, was a Magi, a priest and an astronomer. But unlike my father, who you could see regarded it as a job and nothing more, Melchior's father was passionate about astronomy. And he shared that passion with his son, who had shared it with me. Balthasar, my other cousin, lived miles away in Egypt, but we had always written and he came to visit every summer. The three of us would lie on our backs in the cool of the Persian night and point out the various constellations, using my father's astrolabe.

Balthasar had the dream first. Melchior and I laughed when he told us that he'd dreamt that we would discover a new star, and that the star would lead us to the King of Kings. We told him he was mad. His face fell when we laughed at him and I could see that a little doubt had crept in, but not for long. He pulled himself up to his full height, which I thought was funny because he was the smallest of us. He told us about the dream again and said that he was going to look for the new star and he didn't care what we thought.

Initially, we ignored his mad comments about his dream, but then I had a very similar dream. At first I thought it was just because I was thinking about what Balthasar had said. But it was so vivid. And in the dream I heard a voice call my name.

The following day, Melchior ran up to me and told me that he'd had a similar dream to Balthasar's, but at the end of his dream he'd seen a child. In my dream I'd seen a man hanging on a cross. Balthasar reminded us that in his dream he'd seen a woman with a child. One thing we all agreed on was that we'd all dreamed a star and a journey.

I was going to tell my mother, who loved anything to do with the stars, but I never did. At first I thought it might be my imagination, but then Balthasar, Melchior and I had the same dream, three more times each. Each time the dream was more vivid and urgent than the time before. We'd discuss them and write to each other about them, and we made a pact to study the heavens every night to see if we could see "the Star". We marked out on huge charts all the stars in the heavens, to include all the constellations, from Andromeda to Vulpecula.

My father was pleased I was so interested in the stars. He said it kept me out of trouble.

My mother and father passed away and I became the next Magi in the family. It was funny when people started to come to me for advice. Father had always been the go-to man and now it was me.

Then one day, as I was studying the heavens – to be honest, it was more out of habit than expectation, it had been 50 years since we'd had the dreams, but Melchior, Balthasar and I had never broken the pact – I saw it, a new star. It was massive, and it shone so brightly I thought I must have imagined it. I blinked, but it was still there. I closed my eyes and counted to ten before opening them, it was still there. I had to sit down and catch my breath. Before I knew it Melchior had burst into the astronomy room, only half dressed with his long white hair flying in every direction, shouting, "Did you see it? Did you see it?"

He rushed over to my telescope and looked into it. Not that he needed to, you could see the star clearly enough with your naked eye. It seemed to hang in the sky so close you could almost touch it.

Melchior was now muttering, "It's real. It's actually real." Melchior worked out that the star was moving towards Palestine, the place where we had dreamt that a king of kings and a great prophet would be born.

Then with one voice we said, "Balthasar. We need to go and see Balthasar."

I called for my servant who was also my best camel man and told him I needed him to ride as swiftly as possible to Balthasar and tell him we would meet him at the brow of the hill that would lead us into Palestine. I knew that he would have seen the star and would be preparing to meet us. Balthasar lived closer to Palestine than we did and I knew we would have to hurry.

My wife was very startled when I woke up the whole household and told her I was going to see Balthasar. "Are you mad? At three in the morning? Can't it wait until tomorrow?"

But it couldn't wait. I knew it couldn't wait.

I called my bodyguards and my cooks, my stable hands and my musicians, and I told them that we would be going on a long journey. I needed the camels prepared, they were to fill containers with food, water and wine.

I was just about to leave when I remembered that in my dream a man had been hanging on a cross, so I went to my storeroom and I found the myrrh. It had cost a fortune about ten years ago, but there had been something about its fragrance. I had told my wife it was to be used on my death, but now I was compelled to pick it up. If such a child was being born, then I would give it to him. Something told me he would need the myrrh.

My wife was fussing around, demanding to know what the hurry was. I told her not to worry, I'd be back as soon as possible, but I needed to go and see a child. Well, you can imagine her face. Then Melchior arrived with his entourage. You had to be careful when travelling and I noticed that he had also sensibly brought his bodyguards. I heaved my old body onto the camel. I had made it perfectly clear I needed the youngest and fittest camels. It was going to be a long journey, over a 1,000 miles, and we would only be able to follow the star at night. This would not make the camels happy as they were diurnal creatures, but even at 40 miles a night it would take us almost a month to get to Palestine. Balthasar would be able to go at a more leisurely pace, because he was only half the distance away.

Melchior and I looked at each other and saw our 14-year-old selves making a pact over a dream. Then the camels rose and we were off.

We travelled for two weeks and heard nothing from Balthasar. Then early on in the third week, I could see a cloud of sand in the distance and I knew it was my servant returning. He hadn't even dismounted before I asked him what Balthasar's reply was. He would be waiting for us on the brow of the hill into Palestine.

Ten days later, it was with joy and excitement that we saw him waiting for us. As we rested that night in the camp, we got out our charts and looked at the star that hung above us, almost as if it was waiting for us to finish, we reassured ourselves that the trajectory that we had thought the star was on was still in the direction of Palestine. I told the other two that I would need to sleep that night, that I was too tired to travel and needed to rest. I fell into a deep sleep, only to be woken by a bright light. Melchior and Balthasar were also awake, but no one else, even our bodyguards were asleep. Then the light grew brighter and I heard a voice say, "The star will lead you to the King of Kings, the Saviour of the World, you have been chosen to announce his coming."

Then everything went dark again. Out of the corner of my eye I saw the bodyguards come to. Isn't it funny, the silly things you notice when you're in shock.? We looked at each other and nodded, yes we'd all heard the voice. We roused our entourage and continued. You know, during the whole journey not one of the camels went lame, no one complained. It was as if we'd been energised.

Twenty-seven days later we reached Jerusalem and realised we had no idea where the child might be. The star had indeed guided us to this point, but where exactly was the child.

It was my idea to approach Herod Antipas, as the ruler of Jerusalem. I presumed that he would know where the King of Kings would be born. It was a bad decision, and I heard several years later that after our visit he had killed hundreds of babies because we'd approached him about the child. This has been a heavy thing to live with but at that point we just wanted to see the child, the prophet, the King, and so we went to Herod and explained that we were seeking a child who would be the King of Kings. Herod was affable enough, although I noticed him eyeing up our entourage and I could see his mind calculating. But I wasn't in the least concerned when he expressed interest in our mission and invited us to stay with him upon our return home to tell him where the child was.

We eventually left and continued on our journey, not quite sure where we were going. Then Melchior said we needed to stop so he could do some further calculations. Finally, he determined that we needed to go to Bethlehem. We rested a little but we couldn't settle, so we rose and followed the star. It never left us, it neither waxed nor waned, it stayed constantly above us, throughout our journey.

We eventually found ourselves in a poorer part of Bethlehem town, not at all what we'd expected. As if guided by an invisible hand our camels continued until the star seemed to stop over what looked like a stable. How could a king of kings, a great prophet be born in a stable? Surely not. And where was the singing coming from? It was the most beautiful singing I had heard, it far surpassed my own, very fine musicians. People were looking at us and I could see that my bodyguards were on high alert, but our camels just kept on moving until they reached the stable, with the star shimmering above it casting a silver light. We could hear the gentle voice of a woman singing to a child, a lullaby. One my mother used to sing to me. We looked at each other. People had come out of their homes and were watching us. Slowly we dismounted. What were we doing in front of a stable? Even though at that moment it looked more beautiful than any stable I had ever seen. Maybe Melchior had got it wrong? My servant knocked on the door and when it opened I glimpsed the child for the merest moment. And I knew that the star had led us on this journey to see the King of Kings, a great prophet. True, he was a babe, but even that one glimpse told me of the truth of his being.

The door opened wider and we were invited in, and there were Melchior's and Balthasar's parts of the dream, fulfilled: the child; the mother and child. Then I knew that my part of the dream would also be fulfilled and that this child would grow into a man who would suffer and die on a cross.

As I knelt before the child with a heavy heart I handed him my gift, the myrrh that I knew would be used at his death. How I envied Balthasar's gift of gold, and Melchior's gift of frankincense. The mother was so young, and she looked so worried.

There was flicker of fear in her eyes when I handed her the myrrh, but then she just held the child a little tighter to her.

The star didn't move, so we stayed a while, and found out a little about the girl, Mary, and her husband. He was a carpenter, an honest trade. We told them about our dreams. I didn't mention all of what I'd seen in mine. We told them about the message. The husband, Joseph told us that he too had received a message from an angel.

The child didn't cry once. He must have been about four to six weeks old by now, but the way he focused on us! Never had I seen such concentration in a child of that age – and I've had seven, so I do have some experience. The peace I felt as he gazed upon me was beyond description.

Eventually we left. I would have liked to stay but it would not have been appropriate, and people were beginning to approach our entourage with enquiries. I could see that Balthasar and Melchior were as affected by what they'd seen and experienced as I was.

We left the child and began to travel towards Herod to tell him where the child lay. But then all three of us had an identical dream in which we were warned not to return to Herod, but to go back to our homes another way. When Melchior checked his charts, a new route had been mapped out for us. The marks on the map were not made by Melchior, and no one else was ever allowed to touch his charts.

That was 30 years ago, and I hear that there is a prophet in Jerusalem. Some call him the Son of God and some the King of Kings. I am too old and frail to go and see him for myself, but then I have seen him.

I know this is the child we journeyed to see and my heart breaks a little more each day, because I know the time is coming when my dream will be fulfilled and he will hang on a cross, as innocent as the day I saw him all those years ago.

Singer Deborah Aloba has been teaching singing and music for over 20 years. She managed a small opera company for 12 years and has run opera workshops in schools and prisons.

Her first book, *Teaching Dyslexics How to Read and Write Music*, came from her experience with a diverse student base, which includes students with dyslexia and other learning difficulties – all while acquiring a Master's in Vocal Pedagogy.

Lightning Source UK Ltd.
Milton Keynes UK
UKHW022305161121
394081UK00005B/193